A Closed Volume

AF574991

Dr. Ganesh Janardan Ghugare

ISBN 978-93-5610-747-2
© Dr. Ganesh Janardan Ghugare 2022
Published in India 2022 by Pencil

A brand of
One Point Six Technologies Pvt. Ltd.
123, Building J2, Shram Seva Premises,
Wadala Truck Terminal, Wadala (E)
Mumbai 400037, Maharashtra, INDIA
E connect@thepencilapp.com
W www.thepencilapp.com

All rights reserved worldwide

No part of this publication may be reproduced, stored in or introduced into a retrieval system, or transmitted, in any form, or by any means (electronic, mechanical, photocopying, recording or otherwise), without the prior written permission of the Publisher. Any person who commits an unauthorized act in relation to this publication can be liable to criminal prosecution and civil claims for damages.

DISCLAIMER: *This is a work of fiction. Names, characters, places, events and incidents are the products of the author's imagination. The opinions expressed in this book do not seek to reflect the views of the Publisher.*

Author biography

field experience

Dr Ganesh Janardan Ghugare
As freelance trainer 5 years (Education, Art, Law)
As educational campaigning with Edubridge India platform throughout Maharashtra
As an author, written and published, 6 Books on history and art
As an artist 22 exhibitions
As film makers 26 short films and 3 web series

EDUCATION

MA- HISTORY – 2010 – University Of Mumbai
ATD- ART - 2005 – JJ school of art, Director of Art, Maharashtra Govt., Mumbai
AM- ART - 2009- JJ school of art, Director of Art, Maharashtra Govt. Mumbai
PGDB- HISTORY - 2007 – KJ Sommaiya deemed University

LL.B.- LAW - 2014- University Of Mumbai
PH.D- HISTORY- 2017- JJTU University, Rajasthan

AWARDS AND APPRECIATIONS

Total 18 awards for achievement and contributions in school education sector
Attended many CBSE sessions and international summit
Research paper published in ISSN magazines
Participated national/ international level research conferences

CONTENTS

A blood Story

A blood Story

Mohini and Sushant got married today and Mohini enters the house. Everyone in the house is happy today. Mohini is sent to Sushant's room with a glass of milk.

Today was their first night. Sushant Mohini looks at each other and gets into bed. The night lights are turned off. Exhausted by the rush of marriage, relatives sleep at night. Mohini and Sushant are in each other's arms. Some relatives get up after two in the morning. They start beating and killing the family. Then their views go to Mohini and Sushant's room. Mohini gets up and opens the door. Lallan is standing in front. Sushant is surprised to see them. Lallan Mohini smiles. Sushant is surprised. Looking at Sushant, Mohini hold Lallan's desi gun and shoots him. Sushant gets shot and falls on the bed on the same first night.

In the morning, the local police come and inspect the investigation. It shows them bleeding profusely. After them, it is noticed that there was a wedding ceremony here, but all the bridesmaids are missing. The main thing is that the bride at the wedding was nowhere to be seen. The local police concluded that this was a premeditated attack and that the bride must have taken the door somewhere. Because there have been four such robberies and many murders in the last two or three years.

A month later… ..

Mohini enters his boss's cabin. Her boss in the cabin says he likes to talk about her behavior. And reveals to him his desire to marry her. She nods to him. The kishor demands marriage. He calls Mohini and informs her that his mother agrees to the marriage. In addition to bringing her relatives to plan and confirm wedding function her marriage, the kishor's mother has invited goldsmith at home to select jewellery for mohini. Let her know. Lallan and his gang come to Kishor's bungalow as her relatives. The goldsmith has brought jewellery there. Lallan and his gang kill everyone there. Mohini shoots the kishor in the head.

When the local police re-investigate, they find out that the girl who was supposed to be married after the crime has gone missing.

Many such incidents have taken place in the last two-three years. In which the girl and her relatives get married and then kill the whole family and disappear. As the local police failed in their investigation, the crime branch asked ACP Prakash Rathore, the commissioner, to find the gang and get rid of it.

Lallan and Mohini have a relationship and they go to a hotel room to celebrate their loot and success.

ACP Rathore cross-examines Witnesses of last cases and gathers information and photos of Mohini and Lallan as well as Baja, Khamosh Singh, Pappu and Baban in their gang. ACP Rathod goes to Mohini's house. That's when he realizes she's married. Her husband Sunil is a teacher and she has two daughters. Her husband Sunil says, "She wanted a lot of money and she had sex with Kunal, son of Raghavendra Thakur from the same village for money. She had left my house and moved to Kunal. But after Thakur kicked her out, Lallan gave her shelter. Taking Lallan by the hand, she shot Thakur's son Kunal. She hasn't come back since, and I haven't asked her. "

ACP Rathod goes to Pahadganj to meet her mistress, her father Kantilal. Kantilal says, "Her symptoms were not good. Before the wedding I caught her with some people for money. In order to make her life better, I married her to a teacher with a good boy like Sunil, but she did the same there. She just wanted to make money. Either way. She shot Thakur's son Kunal with one of her lovers Lallan in her hand and then she came here to hide with me. I told her to get out of here, and she died for me. "

ACP Rathore goes to her college to check Mohini's background. ACP Rathore get information that, the professor hear from an alumnus students named Varun, Mohini has been living with him for the last month as he has some difficulty. Varun was Mohini's classmate. ACP Rathore and his team leave for Varun's address.

ACP Rathore meets Varun. So Varun finds out that Mohini has left. The ACP tells him her background and the crimes she committed. So Varun is very shocked. The ACP asks him to look at the safe of the house. When his wife opens the cupboard, all her jewellery and cash are not in place and the cash brought from the land transaction is missing. Varun's brother-in-law Vicky is scared and says that Mohini has left a bag with him.

As soon as the ACP Rathore bag is opened, RDX and time bomb appear inside. ACP lowers the house. How did Mohini get the key to the safe? After checking everyone, ACP becomes suspicious of Vicky. After scanning Vicky's mobile from the cyber lab, he finds his chats and pornographic videos with Mohini. Vicky admits she lured Vicky into her love trap and had a relationship with him and with his help got the key to the locker. Mohini had left the bag with him saying that she had some important items in it. Vicky didn't know it had a bomb in it.

ACP Rathore suspects that Lallan was nowhere to be seen in varun case. So he was sure that the rest of her companions would be around. Accordingly he began to inquire into the lodge. Finally found out at a lodge. Recognized photo of Lallan and companions. All these people were at the lodge and they were ordering pizza. After visiting the pizza shop, Rathore gets the mobile numbers of Lallan and his accomplices. By tracking the mobile number, tracking the location, they start chasing Mohini's Lallan. They know that the police have declared them wanted.

Lallan tells Mohini to move away from this area. But before that, she wants to kill Raghavendra Thakur. Meanwhile, Mohini Lallan and other companions become different. ACP Rathore and the team catch the other comrades in stages and kill them in an encounter.

As soon as Mohini Thakur is called to the field at night, Kunal is not killed by her but by Lallan and she proves that she is stuck in it. She also wants money to hire a lawyer and is willing to have relations with him in return. When Thakur goes to the field, Mohini, tie his hands and feet and kill him. Goes away from there. While tracking Thakur's phone, Rathore traces Lallan's phone and ACP finally encounters Lallan. ACP Rathore catch Mohini and puts a gun to her head. The sound of the bullet revolves.

Lola O Lola

Lola O Lola

The story is from a small town. At eight o'clock in the morning, there was a crowd of people coming for the morning walk and after the morning walk, were enjoying milk tea and green tea, at Bablu Ustad's tea stall. After jogging, Lokesh Lamkhade (LOLA) he was known as LOLA in his friend circle. He sat on the bench with a newspaper in his hand. He picked up the tea. Lokesh Lamkhade, a crime reporter, was observing at his article on today's issue of cheating women and crime against women.

When Bablu Chahavala asked Lokesh (LOLA) why he had not seen him in the morning for the last 10 days, he said he was out of town to work on a project. Lokesh was living alone. His parents died in the accident. His living situation was bleak. He used to get up every morning and having tea at the Bablu’s tea stall at morning.

Lokesh used 2 to give tea and Biscuits every day to the lunatic who was wandering around the stall. He heard from Bablu that a girl named Oshin had come here every morning for 10 days to meet Lokesh (LOLA). Waits for him and leaves. When Oshin arrives and she asks about LOLA, Lola meets her there. Oshin is studying journalism and needs guidance in criminal investigative journalism. Lola promises to help her.

Oshin and Lola begins to meet. Oshin begins to realize that she is in love with Lola. She confesses her love to Lola and proposes him for marriage. As Lola refuses, Oshin pursues him to convince. Sometimes on the street, in the library, hotel, temple, walking with a friend, sometimes in the library she sits in front of him and looks at him. Lola and Oshin are both sitting upstairs and in deep thought. Trees or grass near the steps.

Oshin asks him about marriage. There is no one like her in this world, she hugs Lola to start a new life with each other. Lola is worried about life with meagre earning. He tells Oshin to think again. Oshin gets annoyed and tells him that she will be happy with him. She doesn't want money. Oshin tells Lola that if you have love and want to marry me, he will visit the stall tomorrow. If you don't come, she will leave and will look back once. She leaves with crying eyes. Lola is confused. He loves her, but he does not dare to come into the decision. What to tell her? He hears the call of a girl, Lola .. Lola .... In this question he turns off the table lamp on his writing table. He lost in the thinking. He decides not to meet her the next day and goes to sleep there. 11:30 pm appears in his old watch.

Finally the next day Lola accepts her love. The two get married and the new world begins. One day Oshin calls Lokesh, LOLA. Then Lola is surprised. He hears the call of a girl, Lola .. Lola ..., Oshin says the name is made from the first letter of Lokesh Lamkhade. Lola says it was his nickname in college. One night Lola can't sleep. He hears the call of a girl, Lola .. Lola .... Oshin was fast asleep.

Lola, however, could not sleep. Lola closed his eyes looking at the fan and opened it again. The fan was spinning uniformly. Lola closed his eyes again and fell asleep. Lola opens his eyes, looks at the roof and closes his eyes. But suddenly his eyes open again. To him the roof looks somewhat different. He gets up and sits down. He is in a different place at the moment.

A locked room, there 3 alone. There is no one in the room. There is no Oshin. The room is very dirty and door is strong and closed. There are no windows. The same room has an open toilet. Lola is under surveillance of the camera. Lola has a dream that he rubs his eyes and takes pinches himself to see the truth. He is shocked. He doesn't know how he got here. Lola banged the door against the wall and struggled to get out.

Finally sits on his knees and shouts looking up. Oshin wakes up in the morning. It's too late. She thinks Lola is in the bathroom, he's not there. She searches for him. She finds him around the house. She calls him and the phone is at home. She calls his office but he never comes there. Calls his typical friends. She gets a little irritated and stands near the door. She has tears in her eyes and she is a little angry and worried about Lola's behaviour.

Lola is closely monitoring the place. It was now written 1 day on a nearby white board. He sees that he is being watched through the camera. He throws objects to blow up the camera but the camera is in a net at a height. He gets irritated. Shouts. Breaks objects and pulls the bed sheet and falls unconscious. Oshin goes to the police station. She is very restless.

Police officer Arun Sardar tells Oshin that her husband Lokesh Lamkhade (Lola) has been missing since this morning. Lokesh is well known as he is a crime reporter to Arun Sardar. Oshin says we slept together at night. He was not by her side in the morning. I waited all day and he also left the phone at home. Arun Sardar promises to find him, her husband Lokesh Lamkhade and tells her to go home. Oshin comes out crying.

Lola opens his eyes. He is not well. His head hurts terribly. Even in that situation, he stands up. He is shocked. The luggage, he had torn or whisked had been re-arranged. He understands that someone has come into this room and he is watching me 24 hours a day. It was written on a nearby white board for 2 days now. Lola gets irritated, his anger is unleashed but nothing works.

Lola starts shouting loudly. He asks the question, who are you? Why are you holding me like this? On the 8th day, Lola, who has regained consciousness, sees a plate of food in front of him. Lola slides the plate over and starts eating it. Oshin is alone at home looking at Lola's photo and crying. She asks what went wrong with her and sits down crying. 4 Lola is sitting down. It's been 15 days since the board was on. The lights are on and off.

Lola yells at the light. In that darkness he seems to cut his movements in the blue dim light in the corner. Oshin, meanwhile, makes daily rounds of the police station. Oshin is told by the constable at the police station that there will be a search. Lola falls asleep. Meals are kept. A good meal today is sweet. Seeing Puri and mixture of Kheer - Shrikhand, vegetables makes his mouth watering. Lola thinks, why gave up today? But his appetite does not quench his hunger. Day 100 board appears. He washes his hands in a dish that is finished eating. The dish pushes forward. After eating, he walks around .After a while, he gets a slap on his eye. And he falls asleep and falls down. His head starts spinning. His eyes slowly close Lola slowly opens his eyes.

When he open his eyes, he see a clear sky in front of him. He is lying outside in the forest. His face was cleansed. His clothes were changed and given a new one. He was given a clean bath. He holds his head again. He doesn't know how he got here. He begins to find a way. Starts wandering here and there. As he wanders, he sees a pond or water. Lola goes near the water. He dips his mouth in water and drinks it. While drinking water, he sees a full glass of tea in front of him. He comes to the glass, picks up the glass, looks around and sees another full glass. He comes to the second glass, picks up the glass, and as he looks around, he sees a third full glass. Then he sees the glasses and he keeps track of them as if someone is showing him the way and Lola wants to reach him. At last he sees a desolate house.

Lola guesses the outside of the house and sees a cup of tea in the doorway. He knocks on the door. But the door is tight. Lola decides something with his mind. He picks up a large wooden pole or iron pipe a nearby, and if there is anyone inside, he kicks the door in response to his attack. The door opens inwards. The door opens inwards. Lola comes inside. And stares in amazement. Because this is the room where Lola was stuck.

Lola looks around. But this time he sees a bag on the bed. Lola suspects that there are some explosives inside. He gently opens the bag. Inside there is only an empty glass of tea and a greeting card with the words "Find me". Finding your tea will be crazy but I won't find you. Lola makes a noise under the bed. He is shocked. He sees the bomb below. its minutes are over. Lola runs out. 5 Lola runs out of the house. Looking back, there is a big explosion. He longs to survive the bombing. Lola faints and falls down. The chirping of birds in the forest continues in the light.

Lola's eyes closed. Lola's eyes open and he comes to his senses. The darkness disappears. Lola is lying near his house, he knows the place. He comes close to home. He is in a hurry to meet Oshin. He runs away. Comes near the house and rings the house bell. Knocks on the door. But as he sees name plate of Shri. Manoj Satpute on the door. Lola thinks. Unknown person opens the door and asked him who are you? That person's name is Manoj Satpute.

Manoj Satpute tells him this is my house and I have been living here from the last five years. In the house he sees Oshin and his photo. Manoj says that this is a photo of his wife, Oshin Satpute. Lola is surprised and starts hitting Manoj. Manoj pushes him out of the house and locks the door. Lola goes to Bablu Ustad's tea stall. Bablu Ustad asks him where he was? Oshin tells Bablu that she was looking for him. Lola goes to the police station and meets Arun Sardar and tells him all the facts.

Arun Sardar comes home with Lola. The nameplate on the house door had also changed. There were some changes again in everything inside the house. Oshin was crying at home. She hugs Lola. Lola asks her, there was another person here, when he came here a few times earlier. Oshin denies this.

Arun Sardar leaves and sees the madman on Bablu Ustad's tea stall, calls him and pays him. Oshin tells him that she gives him his favourite mixture of Kheer - shrikhand and puri. Lola notices that he was given a similar dish on the last day of his imprisonment. He didn't like this dish. He once told Oshin that he likes mixture of Kheer - shrikhand on it. The fact that only Oshin and Lola knew only this unique mixture of Kheer – shrikhand.

Lola realize that Oshin did it all. Oshin strikes Lola on the head. Lola regains consciousness. His hands are tied to a chair and his mouth is bandaged. Oshin fills his bag and stands in front of Lola. She confess and explains the reason behind it. She says her sister Nayan Walia was Lola's college friend. Her father had arranged her marriage but she ran away on the wedding day by leaving a letter.

It was written in a letter. I'm leaving with Lola. We are going to get married. Don't find us. Our father was died due to heart attack. The mother 6 suffered a mental shock. She too had been numb like a corpse for 10 months. She's pass away. When Oshin searched for Nayan a lot, she found Lola i.e. Lokesh Lamkhade in Nayan's group. Oshin come to know that Nayan had been with you that night. Oshin did not have any evidence, so both of them were legally mature, so Oshin could not give any punishment by law. A few days later, the police found Nayan's body in accident. She was wearing familiar clothes.

The police did not know about her husband. So Oshin decided to find out and punish him. Oshin cuts off the nubs of Lola's hand. She leaves the house. Oshin gets a call. This call was made by her sister Nayan. Oshin is shocked Nayan tells her that she has come to live in the city next to Oshin. Oshin goes to see her. Oshin tells Nayan a lot about her behavior.

Nayan apologizes to her and told her the fact behind a dead body which informed by police. The dead body was of Nayan's house maid who wears same dress on that day donated by Nayan to her. Nayan introduces her husband. Her husband's name is Lochan Lalchand. Oshin then asks she was married to Lola means Lokesh Lamkhade, wasn't she? Then Nayan says her husband is also called Lola means Lochan Lalchand and Lokesh Lamkhade was a friend in Nayan's college group. Oshin realizes that there were two Lola's in college.

Nayan's group did not know about the affair between Nayan and Lochan Lalchand. Nayan says Lokesh gave her financial help to settle their life. Oshin realizes her mistake and leaves to save Lola. She sees a crowd near her house and miss it. That Lola died. Oshin moves towards the crowd to see the picture, she was continuously crying and sees mad person feeding biscuit tea to Lola.

When Oshin leaves, Lola kicks and blows the vase out of the window. The madman sees it and comes home and saves Lola. Oshin apologizes to Lola. Lola walks away. Everyone leaves. As soon as Oshin picks up her bag, the madman gives her a rose sent by Lola. Oshin runs over and hugs Lola and says sorry.

Aarambh

Aarambh

Raghav and Pari are newly married and moved to a new city where Raghav moved his IT company's office. Pari told her father over the phone how the day goes. Pari's father , Mr Arun Palande Congratulate her. Raghav's parents are not there. The house was well decorated by Pari. Raghav had bought a house of her choice so, she was very happy.

Today there is a lot of work to cover the house so the Pari orders a meal from outside, the meal grows on the dining table and Raghav is at work on the laptop. The Pari asks him to sit down to eat. Pari had ordered Raghav's favourite menu for dinner today.

On the bed, the both of them, chat about their journey from love to marriage. Their journey from their first meet to today. Raghav and Pari fall asleep in each other's arms.

In the Pari's dream, Madan Gopal comes to her with a one-sided lover, who doesn't like her from college. Madan Gopal was a professor in Pari's College. The rude one tries to get close to her. In it his nails touch her wrists. She pushes him away. Suddenly the Pari wakes up. She was aware that, she had dreamed. Madan Gopal was trying to get close to her in her dream. Raghav is fast asleep.

The Pari wakes up Raghav after taking her own bath. Raghav pulls the Pari back into bed. The Pari reminds him of a meeting in his office. Raghav immediately starts preparing to leave.

The Pari fills his lunch box and Raghav fills his office bag and laptop. Raghav goes to work. When she covers everything in the kitchen and washes her hands, she found nail marks on her wrist. She remembers her wrists tightly. When Madan Gopal grabbed her hand, she felt his nails. But her mind is not ready to accept, because how will the wounds of dreams rise on her body?

In another place, Madan makes a drink in front of a photo of a Pari. He also kisses the photo of the Pari and tells her that he is back. Madan makes a peg of liquor, puts the liquor on the lips of the photo and promises to meet her again.

Before going to bed at night, Pari tells Raghav a nightmare on the bed. It also shows injuries to the wrist. Raghav laughs. Raghav explains how the wounds in the dream will come to the real body? Explains that she must have felt by her. When the Pari goes to tell again, Raghav silences the Pari.

It is 3 o'clock at night. The Pari is fast asleep. The Pari wakes up and picks up the water jug to drink water. She sees it empty. She is stunned and comes back to the dining table to fill the water jug. She sees Madan in front of her. He hugs her. Then she pushes him again. Madan gets up and grabs her by the throat and falls down. Madan starts taking bites while kissing her on the Pari's neck, shoulders. The Pari starts screaming.

Madan was flirting with the Pari in a dream. Raghav hears the sound of a Pari crawling. The Pari screams. Raghav wakes her up she is scared. Raghav calms her down by pouring water on her. She says all sorts. The Pari sleeps with her head on Raghav's lap.

The Pari was fast asleep. Raghav's Pari wakes up ready to go to work. The Pari tells Raghav not to go, but Raghav says there is a big business meeting at work. The Pari tells him to cancel the meeting. Raghav tells her he can't do that and promises to call her in the afternoon. The angel knocks on the door. Goes into the bathroom. Brushing teeth. Washes face. When the hair pulls back, the marks of teeth appear on her shoulders. She sits crying under the shower.

In another place, Madan talks about yesterday's type with a photo of a Pari. Madan expresses his sorrow as she did not allow him to kiss her. He hold the photo of the Pari to come near him. Finally kisses her photo.

Raghav comes home. Most of the time, when the Pari does not open the door by ringing the door bell, he opens the door with a duplicate key. The house has a base. Raghav calls the Pari and turns on the light. He sees the Pari sitting in the dark in the bedroom. Raghav calls her on mobile all day, but asks but she has not picked up a call. Raghav moves her and asks loudly as if the Pari is in a trance. She regains consciousness and hugs Raghav tightly and starts crying. She used to tell truth Raghav , behind Madan Gopal. Madan like pari in college, often refusing and proposing the same. Pari and her father , Palande complaint to college administration against Madan Gopal. The Pari says that yesterday Madan Gopal had come to her in a dream and he had tried to rape her.

When Raghav doesn't like what she is saying, she gets irritated and the Pari shows him the marks of Madan's teeth. Raghav reassures her. Raghav tells Pari, tomorrow is a holiday, promise to go out.

Raghav and Pari go to a hotel. She sees Madan in the hotel. He lick the lollipop with vulgar expression to show pari and makes an obscene impression. The Pari approaches Madan and asks why he is doing this. Madan shows that he has done nothing. The Pari slap him. Raghav also stops her.

The owner of the hotel tells Raghav to leave. Raghav doesn't like Pari behaviour. Raghav takes her away. Madan is happy and laughs.

Raghav brings the Pari home and blames her for what happened. She gets annoyed and calls her father (Mr. Palande). The Pari tells her father, that Madan is back and he is bothering her. She tells father all the facts. Palande tells Pari that he will come to visit her after finishing some work and stay with her for a few days. The Pari tells him to come early.

Raghav apologizes to Pari for irritating her. He understands her and promises to take her out for 15 days next month. The Pari is happy. she hugs and kisses him.

Potraj Dombari, who is playing a game on the street, is playing hard. He whips himself and asks for money in the name of God. Madan is standing there waiting for the Pari. The Pari intercepts her in Madan on the street as she goes to shopping. Madan confesses to her that he comes to her in a dream and trying to rapes her. He asks Pari to leave

Raghav and marry him. The Pari refuses. Madan expresses his desire to have sex with her. Irritated at Madan's obscene speech, the Pari starts beating him with the whip in Dombari's hand. Meanwhile, police officer Shelar intercepts her. Madan says he is innocent.

The police take both of them to the police station and also call Raghav. The police conduct a reverse investigation. It is heard police from Madan that pari had slapped him earlier. It is also learned that Madan Gopal was a professor of hypnosis and psychology in her college. He had proposed marriage to Pari while in college but after her refusal he says he never met her.

He said his job was lost due to a complaint from the Pari and her father. Pari says that madan came to her dream and was trying to seduce. Inspector Shelar mocks her and asks Raghav to show her to the doctor. Madan tells the police as well as Raghav that he has no complaint. The police release Madan.

When he came home, Pari Raghav had a quarrel. Just then the Pari's father (Palande) comes. Raghav tells his father How is it possible that what the Pari says? The Pari gets angry and closes the bedroom door.

Madan takes off all his clothes and looks at the wounds on his body whipped by the Pari. Madan heals his wounds and tells the Pari to take revenge.

The Pari closes the bedroom door and falls asleep crying inside. Raghav and Shri. Palande Pari's father talks about the Pari's behavior outside and about Madan Gopal's past. That night the Pari screams. Raghav breakes and opens the door. Then, they are soaked with sweat and beaten in places. Raghav asks Pari what happened. The Pari says that Madan was naked in a dream, he hit her with a belt and was trying to take off her clothes. The Pari was unconscious crying.

Raghav takes her to the doctor. The doctor asks her if this was due to a domestic quarrel or a beating by Raghav. The Pari tells the doctor Chinmayi Thakur that, Raghav loves her very much. She tells the doctor about her dreams and Madan Gopal. The doctor calls Raghav and Palande in private.

The doctor says that the Pari must have had a mental illness and that she may have inflicted these injuries on herself. She tells the Pari to see a psychiatrist. Palande doesn't like the doctor’s suggestion, so he decides to teach Madan, a lesson.

When Palande reports Madan to the police station, Officer Shelar explains how to punish for what happens in a dream. When Madan wipes Palande's eye without the knowledge of the police, Palande slap Madan. Palande says police his daughter Pari has to start treatment, now. Then Shelar mocks Palande. Police officer Shelar tells Palande to leave. Shelar asks Madan, "You are not really involved in this, are you?" Then Madan says he is innocent, start crying.

Raghav takes Pari to his psychiatric friend Jagdish. Jagdish says that if we constantly think of something or keep looking at it, it will come in our dreams. Either it has affected the Pari's mind or Madan is constantly thinking about the Pari. When Raghav asks how all this is possible? Jagdish says that, this world is beyond science. It's all a game of the mind. After coming out of Jagdish's center, Raghav gets a call from Officer Shelar. He comes to the police station and tells Raghav, about Palande, what he did and babbles.

Raghav says pari that, he doesn't like what the Pari's father, Palande. Raghav takes her close and falls asleep as the Pari apologizes for the inconvenience.

The Pari dreams again in which Palande is sleeping. Madan Gopal comes there. In the dream, Madan Palande sits on his stomach while he is asleep and pushes the pillow on palande's face. The Pari tries to intercept. Palande already dies of an attack. That's how Madan laughs. The Pari picks up the vase and strikes Madan.

The Pari wakes up and tells Raghav about her dream. Raghav and Pari come to Palande's room. Palande is dead. In the dream, the vase on Madan's head seems to be cracked. But vase has no blood.

Dr Chinmayi Thakur and the police come. Dr. Thakur is said to raghav, that, Palande dead due to heart attack. The police see the corpse and walk away.

Jagdish give one file to Raghav and says read a file ther is a case like Pari, had in a foreign country. In that case, the man was forced to commit suicide. Raghav takes the file and leaves Jagdish's office. Madan looks at Raghav and Jagdish from a distance.

Madan finds information about Jagdish on the internet in a laptop. He opens his photo and keeps looking at it. Raghav reads the file completely. When he calls Jagdish in the morning, Jagdish does not pick up the phone. Raghav goes to his house to meet Jagdish. There he heard that a cylinder had exploded in Jagdish's house, killing him.

Raghav complains to the police against Madan as a suspect in Jagdish's murder. Shelar says Jagdish's house had four bars on the inside, two on the safety door and two on the wooden door. If Madan goes inside, how will he come out?

Raghav sees Madan hit on the head. He remembers the vase that Perry put in his head. His hand looks burnt. Raghav is convinced that the Pari is telling the truth and Madan is doing all this.

Madan is drinking and saying love. Speaking to a photo of Madan Pari, he confesses that he killed Palande and Jagdish. Madan looks at the photo of the Pari and says that he will have sex with her today.

Raghav tells Pari that he is with her. Based on the file given by Raghav Jagdish, we tell Pari to see each other all day long. Raghav Pari looks at each other all day long. And sleep looking at each other's faces.

The Pari has a dream in which Madan Gopal comes. Madan tries to force Pari. Madan goes to get close to the Pari. That's when Raghav comes. Raghav strikes Madan in the head. As such, Madan falls unconscious. Raghav pours wine on top of him and tells the Pari to burn him. The Pari pours wine on Madan and ignites him by throwing a burning match stick. Madan starts screaming and burns.

Raghav and Pari wake up from a dream in the morning. Get rid of the TV. There is news of strange death .It is Madan's death. Madan's body burns but the clothes, jewelery, shoes remain the same.

Police and journalists are also confused. Inspector Shelar falls into consideration. Journalists confuse police officer Shelar with questions.

The Pari brings coffee for Raghav and sits next to him. The news of Madan Gopal's death makes the two look at each other. The two watch TV with their heads on each other's shoulders.

The Curse Of Patonpada

At night, a team of archaeology department lead by Radhika Prajapati waits for the soul of historic soldier, named 'Shiledaar' near the branch of the cursed river in Patonpada area. The wind blows hard. The noise of whistle is getting louder. This is how the movement of animals in the forest began to increase. The sound of horses' hooves begin to come. Shiledar is appeared by Radhika Prajapati. Quickly he is walked away in front of her. Some team members from Radhika crew fainted, and others vomited. Someone is stabbed, someone is stoned and the whole team is injured. Radhika started chasing Shiledaar. But suddenly she lost her balance and fell. Shiledar disappeared and Radhika fainted.

The head of the archaeology department, Dr. Mohan Prakash immediately called on the Archaeological Department's expert History Researcher and Sign Language, Sadashiv Nagarkar. Dr. Mohan Prakash informs Sadashiv that the government is planned to build shortcut road of 12 km from Bhod to Vishrampur.

The road, 8 km out of it passes through Patonpada and the cursed river area. It's a very wild part. This road will save 9 hours of travel. It is said that the soul of a 'Shiledaar' walks in this forest. No contractor goes to the area to survey the work. The locals are against to build shortcut route passes through Patonpada and the cursed river area. The state government sent the archaeology department to conduct the survey. That's how a team went on a search operation. They also saw there, the Soul of shiledaar. Everyone is in critical condition.

Sadashiv prepares for this mission to unravel the mystery of Patonpada. Radhika Prajapati, the head of the last campaign, requests Mohan Prakash to go with Sadashiv for this campaign.

Sadashiv arrives to village Bhod with his team in a small van. He asks the Sarpanch of Bhod village to suggest a local man for crew, to help them show the road from Bhod to Patonpada through the cursed river. But the Sarpanch is not ready for it. Also no one in the village gets ready. Then Kalu Ramoshi from the village gets ready to show the road till branch of the river and return, for a higher payment.

Sadashiv and his team start moving on the road from Bhod to Patonpada through the cursed river. Everyone has horrible experiences while walking. Someone is chasing, someone is whistling, the sound of animals, bones in the right places on the road. Kalu Ramoshi just brings to the river and gestures with his hand, waits and informs them to go to Patonpada on the other side of the river, and leaves with his reward.

Sadashiv crosses the river with his team. The river has knee-deep water. After crossing the river and a small forest, he sees an ancient temple. This is the temple of Goddess Chandrakala Mata. The idol of the goddess is ancient. There Sadashiv sees handprint in octagon shape at the feet of the goddess, it is as hands of the devotee are touching the feet of the goddess.

This octagonal small platform bears the handprints of the devotee of the Goddess. Next is a small 'Shivlinga' of Lord Shiva and a crematorium on one side. It takes a long time to walk through the distance forest. It would have been evening. Radhika sees the patonpada village in the distance. Everyone heads towards the village.

On reaching Patonpada, Sadashiv meets supremo of Patonpada, named Bapu Karbhari. He tells them to rest in the village pada that night. Sadashiv understands about the temple from Bapu. This temple of Mother Goddess Chandrakala is ancient and after the new moon, the light of the moon is gradually on the full moon full time on the palm of the hand of the devotee of the mother. The goddess was his deity. Sadashiv realizes that this village is loyal to his deity. Sadashiv hears the screams of an old man from inside. He asks Bapu about it. Bapu Karbhari says "he is my grandfather who is 120 years old and he tells stories of treasures like crazy." Sadashiv goes inside to meet him. Bapu takes Sadashiv to his grandfather's old man's room about the miraculous things and history here. The old man was in a very miserable condition. He was telling Sadashiv the story of stone and treasure.

The old man says that this is a very old story. Shiledar used to live in this Patonpada village. He was the caretaker of this village. Our village was inhabited by robbers but Chhatrapati Shivaji Raja came and told our ancestors to stop the robbery. He made our robber ancestors the mawla of Swarajya. We were told to keep the forest. We save people, women and wealth from enemies of swarajya by annihilating them as per the order of the king Shivaji raje and the money was deposited in the treasury of the Swarajya. The king rewarded us with a salary and a compliment.

King Shivaji had put a bracelet of honour around the hands of the Shiledaar. One day, Maharaj raided Surat and looted Aurangzeb's black money. The road through the cursed river was the closest. The enemy could not dare to come this way. The chiefs of the Shivaji maharaj took Shiledaar aside and asked him to hide some heavy treasures in the forest of Patonpada. Shiledar hide the treasure with his chosen faithful companions with a diplomacy. They were guarding the place till the Maharaja's message came. Suddenly, the enemies attacked. The Shiledaar cut the enemy. Shiledar was killed in that battle. When the kings heard the news, they gave his family the sword of the honour and the steward of Patonpada. But when he dies, he walks in the cursed river at night. Bapu tells Sadashiv that, "there is no such thing like as treasure, the soul of shiledaar is moving as caretaker of Patonpada. The old man has gone mad."

Sadashiv with his team sees the temple and crematorium premises in the forest. It then goes into the river branch. There was a frightening silence in the area of the river. Sadashiv wonders why Shiledaar is coming? "Tonight, I would stay in the character of the cursed river and see Shiledar to see if he was right and if so, I would catch him. At night, Sadashiv, Radhika and everyone else sit in silence. At night the sound of horses galloping can be heard. The sound of the whistle also begins to come. The atmosphere was horrible. The sounds of animals also start to come. Shiledar is seen by Radhika again. She follows him. But he gets out of the bush. Sadashiv runs on the path shown by Radhika but finds nothing. Sadashiv observes the bush and meditates on the whistle.

Some people form team are scared, but the sound doesn't stop. Sadashiv chases the sound of the whistle. He sees a big rock there. That stone has cracks. The sound is due to the wind blowing. Sadashiv seems to be stuck in that rut. He pulls out the object with a big shout. It tends to be an old one. The bracelet of Shivaji Maharaj is engraved on it. As soon as he came out, the whistle stopped.

Radhika surprizes to see bracelet. She was carried another bracelet as same as founded one. Shiledaar's wife was pregnant. Her name was 'laachi'. She helped shiledaar to keep treasure safe. She ran during the battle incidence of shiledaar to inform Maratha spy head Bahirji Naik. He moved her to a secret place. She gave birth to a cute baby.

In Swarajya, she became fearless. Per month she received a salary in the Swarajya till her death. Later, Shiledara's dynasty continued to grow. Radhika is one of his descendants.

Sadashiv and his team leave for Patonpada. Halfway through they see a crowd in the cemetery next to the temple of Goddess Chandrakala. Everyone goes there. The old man is dead. Bapu Karbhari sets fire to his grandfather's pyre. Sadashiv comforts Bapu for the death of his grandpa. They look at Bapu and the villagers with strange eyes. Bapu and the villagers tell Sadashiv to stop his search and leave the village so that no one can kill him again.

Sadashiv explains to them that there is no soul. The sound of the whistle coming from the forest was coming towards him as he was stuck in the crack of a large rock. The sound of the whistle made the animals run away from the insects, so there was a terrible sound in the silence. Shiledar was not a soul but a human being because a thorn had fresh blood on the bush where Radhika showed Sadashiv to Shiledar.

Sadashiv saw the mark of Bapu Karbhari's thorn in his side in the cemetery. Sadashiv realizes that Bapu Karbhari was walking around as a Shiledaar. Bapu karbhari shown the bracelet of laachi to Radhika. As soon as Sadashiv and his team left, Bapu grabbed their luggage and found it in it. From this, Sadashiv learns one thing. The people of Patonpada know that the treasure is in the forest and they do not want to let anyone know. Sadashiv asks Bapu Karbhari about treasure. Bapu says the treasure is in this forest and we will not stay without finding it.

Sadashiv pulls bracelet towards him and runs away with the team. Sadashiv had gathered a lot of information, so the villagers rushed to kill him. Sadashiv and Radhika as well as their team come out of Patonpada struggling with them. After reaching the border of Bhod, everyone gets in their van and leaves.

Sadashiv puts both bracelets in front of Dr. Mohan Prakash and says that, "he has not met anything more than this". Radhika Prajapati tells him all the facts. Radhika takes Sadashiv to her home for coffee. There Sadashiv's attention goes to Shivrajamudra. Shiva mudra was formed by connecting two links. The stick was made of stone and the treasure was hidden by them. The first line of Shivrajmudra was directly resembling the temple of Goddess Chandrakala. Near the feet of the Goddess was an octagonal platform resembling Shivamudras. The light of the moon grew brighter and went from the face of the goddess to the sign of the octagonal hand and she was visible in the moonlight.

प्रतिपच्चंद्रलेखेव वर्धिष्णुर्विश्ववंदिि◌ा || शाहसुन ◌ो◌ः शशवस्यैषा मुद्रा भद्राय राजि ||

means

As the moon of Pratipada grows with art, and is worshiped all over the world, so will the worldliness of the seal of Shivaji Maharaj, the son of Shahaji, increase.

In a way, the message on Shivrajmudra was signalling the way to the treasure. Taking out the treasure placed at the feet of the mother would be an insult to the Goddess, sc Chhatrapati Shivaji Maharaj should not have taken it out either. Because the mark of that hand was not tamperec with.

Sadashiv realizes. The treasure is under the octagonal emblem in front of the Goddess Chandrakala.

Introduction

A Closed Volume

A book by Dr Ganesh Janardan Ghugare

Short Stories included

A blood Story

Mohini and Sushant got married today and Mohini enters the house. Everyone in the house is happy today. Mohini is sent to Sushant's room with a glass of milk.

Today was their first night. Sushant Mohini looks at each other and gets into bed. The night lights are turned off. Exhausted by the rush of marriage, relatives sleep at night.

Mohini and Sushant are in each other's arms. Some relatives get up after two in the morning. They start beating and killing the family. Then their views go to Mohini and Sushant's room. Mohini gets up and opens the door. Lallan is standing in front. Sushant is surprised to see them. Lallan Mohini smiles. Sushant is surprised. Looking at Sushant, Mohini hold Lallan's desi gun and shoots him. Sushant gets shot and falls on the bed on the same first night.

In the morning, the local police come and inspect the investigation. It shows them bleeding profusely. After them, it is noticed that there was a wedding ceremony here, but all the bridesmaids are missing. The main thing is that the bride at the wedding was nowhere to be seen. The local police concluded that this was a premeditated attack and that the bride must have taken the door somewhere. Because there have been four such robberies and many murders in the last two or three years.

A month later… ..

Mohini enters his boss's cabin. Her boss in the cabin says he likes to talk about her behavior. And reveals to him his desire to marry her. She nods to him. The kishor demands marriage. He calls Mohini and informs her that his mother agrees to the marriage. In addition to bringing her relatives to plan and confirm wedding function her marriage, the kishor's mother has invited goldsmith at home to select jewellery for mohini. Let her know. Lallan and his gang come to Kishor's bungalow as her relatives. The goldsmith has brought jewellery there. Lallan and his gang kill everyone there. Mohini shoots the kishor in the head.

When the local police re-investigate, they find out that the girl who was supposed to be married after the crime has gone missing.

Many such incidents have taken place in the last two-three years. In which the girl and her relatives get married and then kill the whole family and disappear. As the local police failed in their investigation, the crime branch asked ACP Prakash Rathore, the commissioner, to find the gang and get rid of it.

Lallan and Mohini have a relationship and they go to a hotel room to celebrate their loot and success.

ACP Rathore cross-examines Witnesses of last cases and gathers information and photos of Mohini and Lallan as well as Baja, Khamosh Singh, Pappu and Baban in their gang. ACP Rathod goes to Mohini's house. That's when he realizes she's married. Her husband Sunil is a teacher and she has two daughters. Her husband Sunil says, "She wanted a lot of money and she had sex with Kunal, son of Raghavendra Thakur from the same village for money. She had left my house and moved to Kunal. But after Thakur kicked her out, Lallan gave her shelter. Taking Lallan by the hand, she shot Thakur's son Kunal. She hasn't come back since, and I haven't asked her. "

ACP Rathod goes to Pahadganj to meet her mistress, her father Kantilal. Kantilal says, "Her symptoms were not good. Before the wedding I caught her with some people for money. In order to make her life better, I married her to a teacher with a good boy like Sunil, but she did the same there. She just wanted to make money. Either way. She shot Thakur's son Kunal with one of her lovers Lallan in her hand and then she came here to hide with me. I told her to get out of here, and she died for me. "

ACP Rathore goes to her college to check Mohini's background. ACP Rathore get information that, the professor hear from an alumnus students named Varun, Mohini has been living with him for the last month as he has some difficulty. Varun was Mohini's classmate. ACP Rathore and his team leave for Varun's address.

ACP Rathore meets Varun. So Varun finds out that Mohini has left. The ACP tells him her background and the crimes she committed. So Varun is very shocked. The ACP asks him to look at the safe of the house. When his wife opens the cupboard, all her jewellery and cash are not in place and the cash brought from the land transaction is missing. Varun's brother-in-law Vicky is scared and says that Mohini has left a bag with him.

As soon as the ACP Rathore bag is opened, RDX and time bomb appear inside. ACP lowers the house. How did Mohini get the key to the safe? After checking everyone, ACP becomes suspicious of Vicky. After scanning Vicky's mobile from the cyber lab, he finds his chats and pornographic videos with Mohini. Vicky admits she lured Vicky into her love trap and had a relationship with him and with his help got the key to the locker. Mohini had left the bag with him saying that she had some important items in it. Vicky didn't know it had a bomb in it.

ACP Rathore suspects that Lallan was nowhere to be seen in varun case. So he was sure that the rest of her companions would be around. Accordingly he began to inquire into the lodge. Finally found out at a lodge. Recognized photo of Lallan and companions. All these people were at the lodge and they were ordering pizza. After visiting the pizza shop, Rathore gets the mobile numbers of Lallan and his accomplices. By tracking the mobile number, tracking the location, they start chasing Mohini's Lallan. They know that the police have declared them wanted.

Lallan tells Mohini to move away from this area. But before that, she wants to kill Raghavendra Thakur. Meanwhile, Mohini Lallan and other companions become different. ACP Rathore and the team catch the other comrades in stages and kill them in an encounter.

As soon as Mohini Thakur is called to the field at night, Kunal is not killed by her but by Lallan and she proves that she is stuck in it. She also wants money to hire a lawyer and is willing to have relations with him in return. When Thakur goes to the field, Mohini, tie his hands and feet and kill him. Goes away from there. While tracking Thakur's phone, Rathore traces Lallan's phone and ACP finally encounters Lallan. ACP Rathore catch Mohini and puts a gun to her head. The sound of the bullet revolves.

A book by Dr Ganesh Janardan Ghugare

www.ingramcontent.com/pod-product-compliance
Lightning Source LLC
La Vergne TN
LVHW050426160726
843469LV00041B/1251

* 9 7 8 9 3 5 6 1 0 7 4 7 2 *